ANASAZI

ANASAZI

Leonard Everett Fisher

ATHENEUM BOOKS FOR YOUNG READERS

THE WORLD AT THE TIME OF THE ANASAZI
A.D. 500-1300

500-599
Buddhism introduced in Japan
Manuscript illumination begins in Europe
Decimal system originates in India

600-699
Persians invent windmill
Gregorian chant introduced in Italy
Chess invented in India

700-799
Muslims begin building Great Mosque in Cordoba, Spain
Irish monks complete Book of Kells
Printing begins in China

800-899
Arab treatise on modern algebra
Chinese issue paper money
Charlemagne becomes Holy Roman Emperor

900-999
Chinese write about optical lenses
Eric the Red discovers Greenland
Arabs introduce arithmetic to Europe

1000-1099
Harp introduced in Ireland
Timbuktu founded in Africa
William conquers England

1100-1199
Chinese use compass to navigate
Medical school founded in Bologna, Italy
Chinese develop first rockets

1200-1299
Marco Polo travels in China
Danes create first national flag
Cambridge University founded in England

1300
Anasazi abandon homes

For my granddaughter, Danielle Olivia,
with much love

To Dorothy Francis, friend and traveler,
and with appreciation to Barbara J. Mills,
assistant professor of anthropology, The University of Arizona

Atheneum Books for Young Readers
An imprint of Simon & Schuster Children's Publishing Division
1230 Avenue of the Americas
New York, New York 10020
Copyright © 1997 by Leonard Everett Fisher
All rights reserved including the right of reproduction in whole or in part in any form.

Jacket design by Nina Barnett
Book design by Nina Barnett/Ethan Trask
The text of this book is set in Mrs. Eaves.
The illustrations are rendered in acrylic paint on paper.

Printed in Hong Kong
First Edition
10 9 8 7 6 5 4 3 2

Library of Congress Cataloging-in-Publication Data
Fisher, Leonard Everett.
Anasazi / Leonard Everett Fisher.—1st ed.
p. cm.
Summary: Describes the day-to-day life of the Anasazi Indians.
ISBN 0-689-80737-6
1. Pueblo Indians—Antiquities—Juvenile literature. 2. Southwest, New—Antiquities—Juvenile
literature. [1. Pueblo Indians. 2. Indians of North America—Southwest, New.] I. Title.
E99.P9F56   1997
979'.01—dc20
96-26642

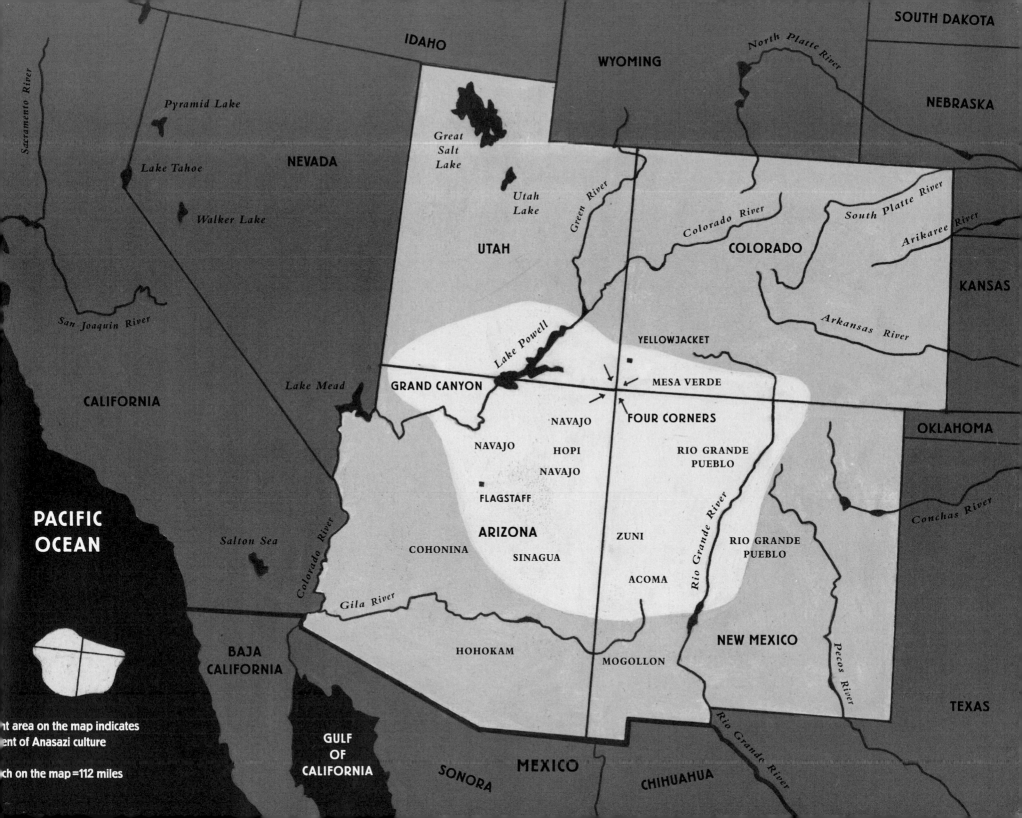

SOUTH DAKOTA

IDAHO

WYOMING

North Platte River

NEBRASKA

Sacramento River

Pyramid Lake

NEVADA

Great Salt Lake

Lake Tahoe

Utah Lake

Green River

Colorado River

South Platte River

Arikaree River

COLORADO

KANSAS

UTAH

Walker Lake

San Joaquin River

Arkansas River

Lake Powell

YELLOWJACKET

CALIFORNIA

Lake Mead

GRAND CANYON

MESA VERDE

NAVAJO

FOUR CORNERS

OKLAHOMA

NAVAJO

HOPI

RIO GRANDE PUEBLO

Salton Sea

NAVAJO

Conchas River

FLAGSTAFF

Colorado River

ARIZONA

ZUNI

Rio Grande River

RIO GRANDE PUEBLO

PACIFIC OCEAN

COHONINA

SINAGUA

ACOMA

Gila River

HOHOKAM

NEW MEXICO

BAJA CALIFORNIA

MOGOLLON

Pecos River

TEXAS

GULF OF CALIFORNIA

SONORA

MEXICO

CHIHUAHUA

Rio Grande River

nt area on the map indicates
ent of Anasazi culture

ch on the map = 112 miles

They had no particular name, at least none that we know of. They were hunters, farmers, basket makers, potters, and house builders. Descended from ancient hunters and gatherers, they drifted chiefly into the steep canyons of the Four Corners region—where the present-day state borders of Utah, Colorado, New Mexico, and Arizona meet—and fanned out elsewhere in the American Southwest about two thousand years ago.

They left the area almost two hundred years before Christopher Columbus set foot in the Americas. In time, long after they had gone and long after Europeans had explored the area, they and their ancestors came to be known as the Anasazi, a Dinneh or Navajo word meaning "ancient ones" or sometimes "ancient enemies."

Who were these people? What were their lives like? Where did they go? Whose enemies were they? The tools, weapons, houses, baskets, pots, bits of clothing, animal and human bones left behind give us some information about them. But the history of the Anasazi from beginning to end still leaves much to be explained. The Anasazi had no horses. No pack animals. No wheels. Yet they built straight roads—thirty or forty feet wide and fifty to sixty miles long—that connected some of their far-flung villages.

They left no written record of themselves other than petroglyphs—carved images on building walls, boulders, and cliffs—and flat, decorative murals. These pictures showed the rabbits, bighorn sheep, and other wildlife they hunted. At times, the Anasazi included human figures in their designs—probably themselves.

The Anasazi stalked deer, antelopes, rabbits, turkeys, and squirrels for food using clumsy wooden spears tipped with stone arrowheads. They also wove sandals, blankets, and baskets from plant fibers. Their weaving method, which produced a twill, or diagonal appearance in the weave, was not much different from twill woven baskets today. The baskets were waterproofed with a tar-like substance and used for cooking, carrying water and cooking stones, or storing food.

These ancient people probably wore next to nothing throughout the blistering summers. But they fashioned animal skins, bird feathers, and plant fibers into clothing to cover themselves during the rest of the year. They also wove cloth from the soft, white, downy cotton plant. Leftover animal bones were made into a variety of tools for scraping hides, cutting and sewing pelts together, or drilling holes in wood and soft stone. Some hollowed-out eagle bones are thought to have been used as flute-like musical instruments.

About the year 500, many Anasazi began abandoning their canyon homesites to join others who had settled onto the scrubby, sun-flooded plateaus to make newer homes among the pines and junipers.

Centuries later, Spanish adventurers in the Southwest would call these high, flat hilltops *mesas*, or "tables."

Those Anasazi living on the fertile plateaus first cleared the mesas with their stone axes. They cultivated the land with nothing more than a trowel-like stone attached to a wooden staff. While they still hunted—now with a more efficient bow and arrow rather than with a clumsy spear—farming slowly overtook their old way of life. They grew corn, squash, and beans.

Anasazi women continued to weave baskets. But they made fewer of them. They preferred clay pots. These they had first seen among mountain-dwelling people who farmed the valleys of east central Arizona and west central New Mexico, and Sonoran desert farmers of northern Mexico and southern Arizona, both with whom they had long traded. The mountain people were later called Mogollon after a Spanish governor, Juan Ignacio Flores Mogollon. The desert people were called Hohokam, or "those who have gone before" by their descendants, the Pima Indians.

Anasazi women learned to fire their own dull gray clay pots and bowls which eventually replaced baskets for cooking, carrying water, and storage. They decorated them with handsome black, red, and white designs over vivid white, orange, and red backgrounds.

The first shelter built by the Anasazi was a pithouse. This was little more than a square, roofed-over hole or pit dug a foot or two into the ground like a sunken living room. They dug a shallow firepit in the center and scooped out a bin at one edge of the dirt floor to store food or possessions. Another hole, which the more recent Hopi people call a *sipapu,* was drilled into each dirt floor away from the firepit. This is thought to have been the entrance to the spirit world.

A low roof of sticks and brush held up by thick corner poles covered the sunken space. Walls were formed by leaning thinner poles against the roof. All of this was covered with a layer of mud dried hard by the sun and winter cold. An opening was left in the roof's center just above the firepit. A wooden ladder was thrust through the opening which served as both the pithouse doorway and a vent to let out smoke from the fire. Air coming into the pithouse was deflected from the fire and kept circulating by a small, low mud wall built a few feet from the firepit. This was a very primitive form of air conditioning.

These sunken pithouses, however, were damp and all too often caught fire. By about 750, the Anasazi had built safer, better ventilated mud-and-pole houses entirely above ground. Several of these houses were attached to each other. And groups of these attached houses formed villages. Spanish explorers, who came upon these villages long after they had been abandoned, called each of them a *pueblo*, their word for "community."

The villages continued to maintain a single pithouse centrally located at the village front. One can only guess that the purpose of the solitary pithouse with its sipapu was ceremonial or religious—an enclosure set aside by the Anasazi to give expression to their spiritual nature. Similar underground structures, which the Hopi call *kivas*, gradually emerged among the later Anasazi generations.

About the year 1000, the Anasazi turned away from the mud-and-pole house construction on the mesas. They began building houses out of skillfully cut stone blocks and sun-dried mud bricks reinforced by sturdy beams hewn from juniper trees. These houses were stronger and more complex than any previously known shelter. They were cooler in the dry summer heat, warmer in the damp, cold winters, and not likely to be burned down by interior fires or torn down by invaders.

The Spanish called these houses *adobe,* a word derived from the Arabic *al toba,* meaning "the brick." Some of them were two, three, or five stories high; their walls double thick. A number of them had fifty to eighty small rooms to shelter a hundred or more people, their belongings, and pet dogs.

Between 1000–1200, several thousand communities lived on the mesa in the southwest corner of Colorado—present-day Mesa Verde—and scattered elsewhere across the American Southwest. One community alone near Yellowjacket, Colorado, had a population of nearly four thousand people living in a series of towers containing 1,826 rooms. There were at least several hundred individual Anasazi communities in and on the Grand Canyon's enormous expanse. It is entirely possible that the total number of "ancient ones" in the region had reached some one hundred thousand people. This would also include the Mogollon and Hohokam peoples, and other Anasazi trading partners such as the Cohonina, far to their west, and the Sinagua, "without water," south of present-day Flagstaff, Arizona.

By this time, the Anasazi had become very dependent for their food supply on what the land produced. The quantity of corn, squash, beans, and wild berries the land gave up and the quantity of small game may not have been enough to feed the growing population that crowded the mesas. Farming was not easy work in a climate as alternately hot and dry and cold as that in which the Anasazi lived. Centuries of farming the same land no doubt drained the soil of its productivity.

Between 1200–1250, many of those Anasazi who had lived on the mesas returned to the steep canyons of their ancestors to live. They climbed down from the open land of the plateaus and built elaborate apartment-type houses in the shelter of the overhanging cliffs. They left the mesa top for farming, clearing fresh lands to improve their yield.

Whether this move was made on behalf of their farming needs is not known. It is possible the Anasazi sought protection against marauders or the weather. Perhaps they wanted to spiritually reconnect with their canyon-dwelling ancestors. There is no evidence indicating any of these reasons, but whatever the cause, the Anasazi worked their land, nimbly climbing up and down the canyon walls using ladders or notches hacked into the stone. Living among the cliffs was risky. Crutches have been found among Anasazi ruins, perhaps indicating that falls were not uncommon.

The cliff houses varied in size according to the height and width of the alcove in which they were built. A low alcove ceiling together with a small floor space would end up in a single-story, one- or two-room house. Some alcoves were so large the Anasazi were able to build two-hundred-room multilevel structures within their space. For the most part, the cliff houses were set back from their ledges to form open courtyards. Here, all of the community's activities—cooking, toolmaking, sewing and weaving, potterymaking, and the like—took place.

The cliff houses were built of sharply cut sandstone blocks cemented together with a mortar made of mud and water. Some of the structures were tall, straight, and rectangular. Others were tall, round towers. All of them were soundly constructed and efficient. Many of the houses faced south, taking full advantage of the warming sunlight in the winter, and of the cooling shade in the summer when the sun was directly overhead. Interior walls, often quickly blackened by small fires, were plastered with a layer of mud and sometimes decorated with designs. Some outside walls also received a layer of mud that dried to a smooth, hard finish.

While the cliff houses rose above the alcove floor, the circular, ceremonial chambers or kivas were dug below ground, below the courtyard. Like the kivas of old, these were covered over with wood poles and mud and had a rooftop entry. And as before they had a firepit, air deflector, and sipapu. But unlike the older kivas, these on the alcoves had built-in stone benches and a separate shaft to ventilate the smoky air.

One can only guess what took place in the kiva: praying, storytelling, healing, teaching, or special meetings. Perhaps it was from the kiva that Anasazi men were sent on their way with a blessing to trade with people in Mexico or on the Pacific coast. Shells and ornaments have been found among the Anasazi ruins that could only have come from these regions. Maybe Mexican and Pacific coast traders found their way to the Anasazi.

Around 1300, a strange thing happened. The Anasazi mysteriously left the Four Corners area. Where did they go? What happened to them? There is no sign that they fell victim to any violence or disease—although skeletal remains show them to have long suffered from arthritis and bad teeth. There are no signs of war, earthquakes, floods, meteor strikes, fires, tornadoes, or plagues. There are not even any significant burial grounds to suggest that they suddenly died off in great numbers.

There was one element, however, that could have played a large role in the Anasazi's move: drought. Over a period of twenty-five years, a changing climate had swept across the northern perimeter of the Southwest. It had become dryer, colder, and hotter by turns. The growing season had become shorter, limiting the amount of food the Anasazi could produce. Between 1276–1299, a waterless period fell on the region. With hardly any rainfall, and the rivers and streams drying up, the Anasazi, in all probability, struggled with unproductive land. They could have arrived at the brink of thirst, famine, and starvation. Their only choice would have been to leave the canyons and migrate to more hospitable places.

No doubt, some of the Anasazi perished far from their origins, having either been judged enemies and turned away by unfriendly people, or fallen victim to the elements. Others were more fortunate. Many scholars believe that they found refuge among various peoples thriving along the Colorado and upper Rio Grande Rivers, mixing their traditions with those of their hosts. Some of the Anasazi migrants joined the Hohokam and Mogollon people who would themselves disperse and seek refuge among other peoples around 1400.

All of these hospitable communities absorbed some of the Anasazi traditions. Four of these cultures—the Hopi, Zuni, Rio Grande Pueblo, and Acoma—are thought to be the principal descendants of the Anasazi. Among these people there can be found a glimmer of the farming, pottery, and housebuilding skills, the pueblos, kivas, sipapus, and general lifestyle that began with the "ancient ones" long ago.

In the end, only the silent remains of the cliff houses in the mesa canyons bear true witness to the Anasazi and their once flourishing civilization.